MUSLIM CHILDREN'S LIBRARY
Muslim Nursery Rhymes
*Author* Mustafa Yusuf McDermont
*Cover/Book Design and Illustrator* Terry Norridge-Austen
CD *Performed by* Harun Abdullah Coombes

*Published by*

THE ISLAMIC FOUNDATION,
Markfield Conference Centre, Ratby Lane, Markfield,
Leicestershire LE67 9SY, United Kingdom
Email: publications@islamic-foundation.com,
Website: www.islamic-foundation.com

Quran House, PO Box 30611, Nairobi, Kenya
PMB 3193, Kano, Nigeria

Distributed by Kube Publishing Ltd.
Tel: +44(0)1530 249230, Fax: +440)1530 249656
Email: info@kubepublishing.com

A Cataloguing-in-Publication Data record for this book is availiable from the British Library

ISNB: 978-0-86037-563-0

*Printed by* IMAK, Istanbul, Turkey

# Muslim
# Nursery Rhymes

Mustafa Yusuf McDermont

Illustrated by Terry Norridge-Austen

THE ISLAMIC FOUNDATION

# 1. Hush a Bye Baby

Hush a bye baby, so pure and small,
He created you, created us all.
Hush a bye baby; you've no need to fear,
We're never alone, when Allah's so near.

Hush a bye baby, breathing so calm,
He will protect you and keep us from harm.
Hush a bye baby, still and serene,
You are a Muslim, Islam's your *Deen*.

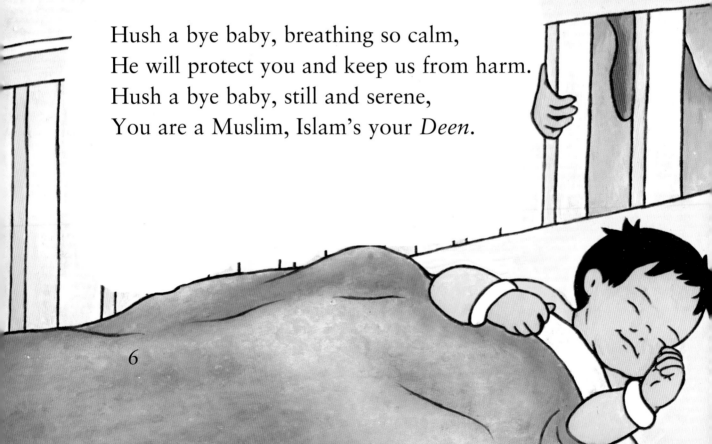

6

# 2. You are a Muslim

Rock a bye baby,
Your cradle is green.
You are a Muslim
Islam's your *Deen*.
Allah's the Lord
His word is Qur'an.
Muhammad His Prophet,
Last Messenger to man.

# 3. Silver Star

Brightly shining Silver Star,
Who has made you as you are?
Sparkling over land and sea,
High above the highest tree.


Allah made you, He made me
Created all so perfectly.

# 4. Little Pony

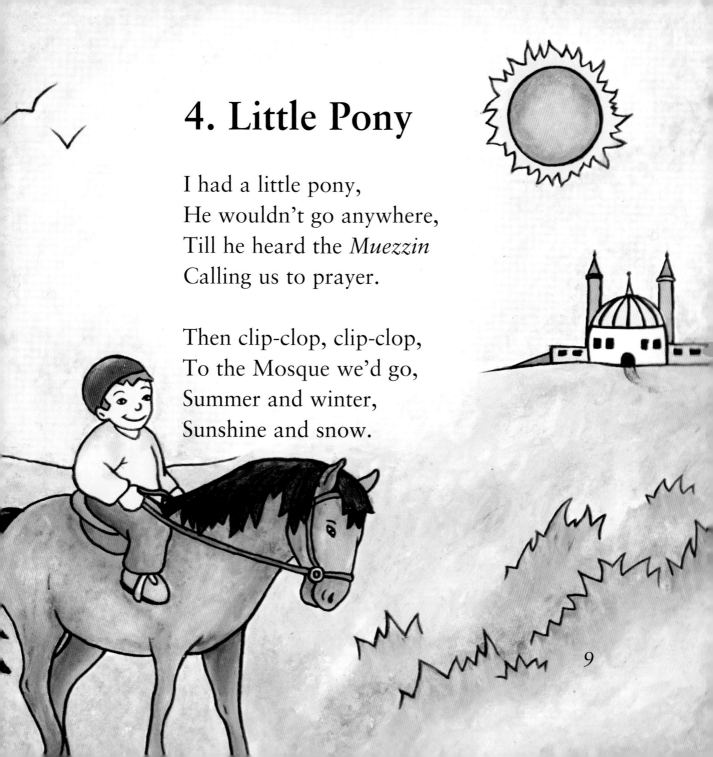

I had a little pony,
He wouldn't go anywhere,
Till he heard the *Muezzin*
Calling us to prayer.

Then clip-clop, clip-clop,
To the Mosque we'd go,
Summer and winter,
Sunshine and snow.

9

# 5. Adhan

Muhammad Hassan!
Come call *Adhan*,
Come call *Adhan*,
And bring Muslims to prayer.

Bring them from factory,
School and home.
Call them to prayer so that none is alone.

10

Call them in the morning,
The noon and the night,
Call them to Islam
To prayer and the light.

11

# 6. Boys and Girls It's Time To Pray

Boys and girls it's time to pray,
*Adhan* is called five times a day.

Stop you're playing or leave your sleep,
Ignore the noises in the street.

Pack up your toys and leave your games,
Remember Allah, Most Glorious of names.

Come in a hurry, come clean and smart,
Speak to your Maker and open your heart.

Praise and thank, Him, All day long
And say you're sorry if you've done wrong.

He'll forgive and give you the power
To think and do good each second
and hour.

13

# 7. Baby Amina

Baby Amina climbed up the stairs;
Baby Amina fell over some chairs.

She tumbled and rolled and started to cry,
But no one could stop her, they tried and
they tried.

Till Sister Khadijah began her prayers;
Then Baby Amina laughed at the chairs.

So if you're so silly to fall down the stairs,
Remember Khadijah just saying her prayers.

15

# 8. Three Good Boys

Three good boys,
Three good boys.
See how they pray,
See how they pray.

They pray together
In a straight line;

And follow the *Imam* in
perfect time;
It's praying to Allah they
truly enjoy
They're three good boys.

16

Three good boys,
Three good boys,
See how they pray,
See how they pray,

They listen and pray without making a noise,
Thinking of Allah they forget their toys;
So sweet are their prayers, they bring them joy
They're three good boys,
Three good boys.

17

# 9. Fatima! Fatima! Where Have you Been?

Fatima! Fatima! Where have you been?
I've been to *Madrassa* with Nur-ud-din.

Fatima! Fatima! What did you do there?
We learned to be Muslims and all about prayer.

Fatima! Fatima! What time do you attend?
We're going next Saturday at quarter to ten.

Fatima! Fatima! Can I come with you?
Yes, of course, you're most welcome, too!

# 10. Where Are You Going To, Omar Abdullah?

Where are you going , Omar Abdullah?
I'm going to London, *Insha-Allah*

How are you going, Omar Abdullah?
I'm going by train, *Insha-Allah*.

What will you do there, Omar Abdullah?
I'll going shopping with Aisha, *Insha-Allah*.

What will you buy, Omar Abdullah?
Clothes and food and toys, *Insha-Allah*.

You are a good boy, *Al-hamdulillah*.
I hope you enjoy yourself, *Insha-Allah*.

But just remember when you return
To give thanks to Allah for all you've
brought home.

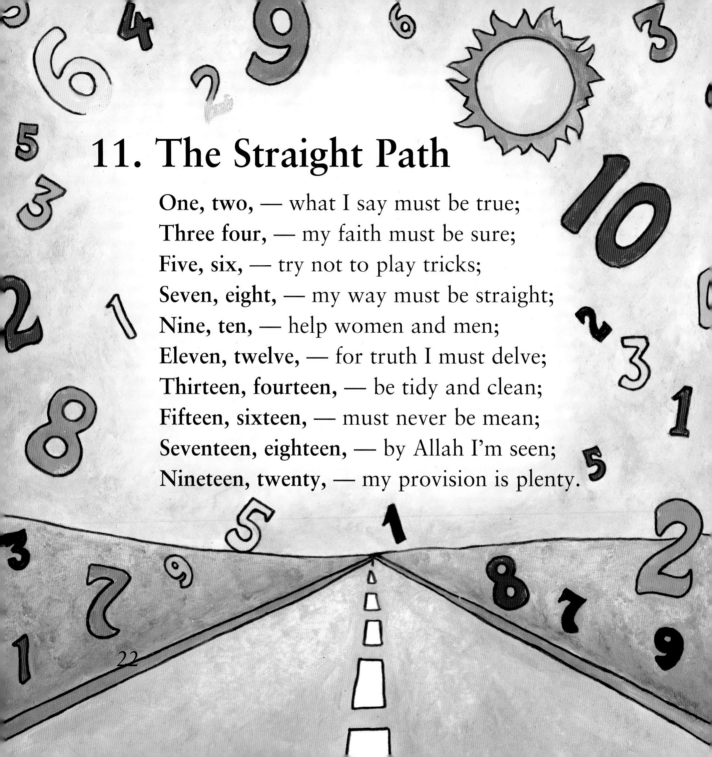

# 11. The Straight Path

One, two, — what I say must be true;
Three four, — my faith must be sure;
Five, six, — try not to play tricks;
Seven, eight, — my way must be straight;
Nine, ten, — help women and men;
Eleven, twelve, — for truth I must delve;
Thirteen, fourteen, — be tidy and clean;
Fifteen, sixteen, — must never be mean;
Seventeen, eighteen, — by Allah I'm seen;
Nineteen, twenty, — my provision is plenty.

# 12. Bread Man! Bread Man!

Bread Man! Bread Man!
Have you any bread?
Yes son! Yes son!
Three rolls left;
One for your family,
One for your school and
One for the poor old man
Who lives with his mule.

23

# 13. When Saleem Made a Promise

When Saleem Al-Amin made a promise,
He didn't make it from matchbox or straw,
He made it like steel, and very very real;
He made it to himself,
He made it to his friend,
Above all – He made it to Allah.

24

He made it to keep, so it never would break.
Come high wind, volcano or even earthquake.

# 14. The Muslims are Coming!

*La-ilaha-illal-lah*
The Muslims are coming.
They've been before,
They're bringing Islam
To every door.
*La-ilaha-illal-lah*
The Muslims are coming
By day and by night;
They tell what is wrong,
And say what is right.
*La-ilaha-illal-lah*

The Muslims are coming
With a message for man;
Allah's the lord,
True guidance - Qur'an
Muhammad the Prophet,
Allah's Messenger to Man.
*La-ilaha-illal-lah*
*Muhammadur-Rasulullah'*
*Allahu Akbar!*

27

# 15. Go Forward, Young Muslims!

Go forward young Muslims
Wherever you are;
In the shadow of the sun
Or by the light of a star;
Your Supreme Protector is
Almighty Allah.
Go forward young Muslims,
Whoever you are;
Press forward and forward
To the light of Allah.
And repeat and repeat,
*Al-hamdulillah!*
*Al-hamdulillah!*
*Al-hamdulillah!*

28

# GUIDES FOR THE TUNES

3. 'Silver Star' based on *'Twinkle Twinkle Little Star'*

4. 'Little Pony' based on *'I had a Little Nut Tree'*

5. 'Adhan' based on *'Little Boy Blue'*

6. 'Boys and Girls, It's Time to Pray'
based on *'Boys and Girls Come Out to Play'*

7. 'Baby Amina' based on *'Humpty Dumpty'*

8. 'Three Good Boys' based on *'Three Blind Mice'*

9. 'Fatima! Fatima! Where Have You Been?'
based on *'Pussy Cat, Pussy Cat, Where Have You Been'*

10. 'Where Are You Going To, Omar Abdullah?'
based on *'Where Are You Going To, My Pretty Maid?'*

11. 'The Straight Path' based on *'One, Two, Buckle My Shoe'*

12. 'Bread Man! Bread Man!' based on *'Baa, Baa, Black Sheep'*